I Thought About You Today

I Want U Now!!!

Stories By

Vincent Tyler

Rose Petals Publishing

I Thought About You Today

I Want U Now!!!

ISBN 0967027209

For information concerning readings for **Book Clubs**
or private parties address inquiries to:

Vincent Tyler
Rose Petals Publishing, Inc.
P.O. Box 378373
Chicago, IL 60637

773.651.0631
ChcCookies@aol.com

This Book Is Not For The Inhibited!!!

There is something to be said for fantasies. We all dream of that perfect person who can satisfy all our needs and desires.

Through his writings, Vincent Tyler has provided a specimen of a man who can court us, love us, and leave us totally satisfied all within his words of his stories.

He wraps you into each and every line, building your hunger, fueling your passions, and romanticizing your mind while taking you on a place of climatic pleasures.

Vincent Tyler has enhanced the art of spiritual sexuality by taking us to a place where our mind and soul is stimulated with the written word.

The sensuous writings of Vincent Tyler are so eloquently presented that women are finding absolute pleasure reading his works.

Sunshine

Contents

*dedicated to all the positive spirits in my life
who encouraged, inspired, supported,
and continued to see in me*

*I am
because of you*

I Thank You

I Hate To Love You

A secret love-hate relationship
I want you out of my life, but I don't won't
you to go

Only You Can Make It Right

Inspired by the song "Two Occasions "
which was written by the magnificent
songwriter, Kenny "Babyface" Edmonds

What Is It...?

There is definitely something about you...
I just can't put my finger on it

Use Me

With total surrender, I give my all to you
Please Use Me

Rose Petals?

If only you would let me take a couple
days just to focus on you

One Kiss

For just once to taste your sweet lips
Tyme isn't an issue

You Make Me Feel

You ignite the soulfire inside of me
You remind me to feel

Pillow

Hurry back!!!

I Thought About You 2day

I'm ready to put my thoughts to practice

Your Passion

It's what keeps our relationship going strong

Here and Now

Behold, beauty at rest

Chocolate Cookies

She is the ultimate

So Happy

Just because you are you

Voyeurism

The bedtyme fantasy come true

Soul Sista

She brings out the very best
in everything that is me

The Choice Is Yours

Whatever you want, just say the word

Did You Like?

Naughty novice

Missing You This Summer

And every summer since hasn't been the same

My Brand New Love Seat

December 17, 1998
7654

Bon Appetite

A use for every item...
Good Eating

Psychoanalysis 3

In the Psychoanalysis series,
Tyrus finds himself in another odd position
as he does in every story

Brown Eyes

Oh, yes you are

lend me your imagination

I Hate 2 Love U
(Damn, it Feels Good)

Oh what a heavy weight it is on a man
to be so deeply in love with a woman he can't stand

we don't get along
we don't see things the same

its rare that I even speak to you
I cringe when I hear your name

people say that we should talk it out
but I know it wouldn't do us any good

baby I hate 2 love you
but it feels so good

I try my best to avoid you
I try to clear u out of my mind

I don't like for you to call me up
so please stop wasting your tyme

because as soon as I hear your sweet voice
that's when I know you're up to no good

baby I hate to love you
but it feels so good

after we do this one last tyme
I'm gonna do you like I should

cause um about to dump your ass
anybody with good sense would

baby please don't kiss me there
you know that makes me feel so... c'mon

baby I hate to love u
but it feels so good

how could it be that I enjoy the hands
of a woman can't stand

Only You Can Make It Right
(With All My Heart)

desire's burning so hot 2nite
if you don't hurry I'll go out of my mynd
so rush on over
close to my side

only you can make it right

I need your lips whispering songs to me
the soft of your body laying here next to me
I need to share your passion
your ecstacy

only you can make it right

I want you to take me to places others fear to tread
we can use every inch of this king-size bed

only you can do those things to me
you go straight to my head
until I'm high as a kite
sometymes you make me feel I could fly

only you can make it right

cause every tyme I close my eyes
I think of u

and every tyme I close my eyes
I discover something new

I'm almost to the point where I believe in you
with all my heart
and I wanna be with you
and only you

at the height of passion
I breathe with you

and we breathe together

in the darkness I can see you
and feel you
and fill you

and I wanna be with
because something inside of me
hold close to something inside of you

so close to you

I don't understand this
I don't know the reason why
but I need you now!

I need you right now

2nite

only you can make it right

What Is It...?

it stems from deep in my mynd
it digs to the core of my soul

it is you
it is your passion

it strokes gently my heartstrings
it's the touch of your fingertips burning me

my goodness
you keep me deep in heat
deep in heat

your passion

it gives me the true essence of ecstacy
as your warm waves make me sway

I wonder if I prayed for an answer
would you still kiss me that way

the way that I hunger for your kiss
throughout the day

would you kiss me the way that you do
to set that fire burning inside of me

that fire inside of me that burns for you

your passion

because in my mynd there is no concept of tyme
there are only the things you are giving me

the things you have given me

and the endless greed for you that has taken over me

if I could I would
take you
taste you
then overdose on you

suddenly you have become my deity
and I fall before you
with humble heart
down on my knees

what is it in you that has taken over me?

what could it possibly be?

your passion

Use Me

do you enjoy me
the same way that I am enjoying you

the same way that I am enjoying this whole experience
with you

don't be afraid to

use me

exploring you

meeting your soul

sharing your vibe

caressing your softness

passion filling inside

use me

use me to get where you wanna go
and as long as it feels good to you
I'll keep riding in the groove

use me

use me to reach that pleasure which you long for
any way that would you like me to do it
for as long as you like for me to keep doing it

use me

if you can dig it
I can definitely get with it

use me

make me your joyride this tyme
so I can feel you shifting gears
into overdrive

use me

zero to ecstacy in the heat of a flash
straddle this young-buck stallion

cruising on your mustang 6.9

use me

practice new positions with me
keep it hot   keep it sweet

use me

don't be afraid to try with me
things that you may consider to be indecency

things that if you ever tell your friends
for they might start look at you differently

so to be on the safe side
we can just keep it between you and me

us two
us three
or
us four

use me

use me to escape from all of that mess
mental anguish and stress
play with my mind
put my body to the test
choose me

use me

Rose Petals?

I envision the farthest reaches of galaxies
and the dust that remains in the wake of
shooting stars

but there's no better sight than watching you
lower yourself into the warmth of the bubble bath
that I have prepared for you

I've always liked watching you do that
I guess it's a personal thing with me

so now I'm on my knees
at your side

I take my tyme to bathe you
dipping the sponge into the warm water
and wetting your skin as it flows in trails down your
backside
like soapy waterfalls
or little white rivers

I'm careful not to get your hair wet
as you lay back and play with the rose petals in the
tub

under the water I find your legs
I focus on your sensitive spots

my fingers wrap around your ankle
raising your left leg from the water and to my mouth

shamelessly I place a kiss on the side of your little toe
and then on all in between
until I work my way over to the big one

my tongue runs from the bottom of your foot
then to the heel and alongside the ankle
not really caring that the water is quickly streaming
from your foot
to my chin

I press my face harder to the soft-bottom
licking the arch
inadvertently tickling you

I'm such a junkie for the vibes you give me
ooh you bring it out in me

and then after a few more glasses of wine

I dry you off and lead you to the bed
right about the tyme the wine has gone to your head

immediately treating you to an oil massage
insuring that no part of your body goes untouched
covering every inch of you until your skin is
completely coated with its scent

then softly
softly your fragile body melts in the hold of my big
hands
as I manipulate you with selfish motives
like those 2am unfinished dreams
when I awake from my sleep with an intense hardcore
appetite to share your desires
it's a vicious hunger to taste your wetness on the tip of
my tongue

in innocence my only intention is to know you much
better than the first tyme

then at the slightest contact
my cup of fantasy spills for you in constant flow
I reach for you
trying not to wake you from your sleep
I plant a kiss on the side of your sleepy face while you
rest
I told you once before

that if you feel me in your dreams
you just keep right on dreaming baby

do you remember when I told you that

so I dive down deeper to taste sweet temptation
that orders me to know the long groove running down
the center of your Sweetback as you meditate on this
seduction
as smooth as a Maxwell track

and again you experience the feel of my strength as
your body envelopes it
in the heat of your...soft
softly
you feel me
measured in inches
don't you

advancing
covering each nipple with wet kisses
and then when lightly blowing upon them

stretching that right leg high into the air
and lightly nibbling at the back of your calf and thigh
stopping only for a moment
to wonder if you notice the chills surfacing on your
skin or if you can feel the reason why

would you mind if I eased my way further south
using my mouth to cover you with sustained laps

now were doing this slowly

you're sprawled across the cool sheets smiling
your eyes closed and your mind open wide
to all of the things that takes place in our naughty little
world

rotating your hips and giving in completely to the
mood
offering me all the fruits of your basket
the sweets of your erotic fruit

if I tried to talk right now I know my words would be
muffled
so instead I listen

and I can her you mumbling the words and songs
of a distant lover's cries and sighs
and
"ooh's and ah's and Oh, my God's,
and keep it right there,
baby please don't stop"

I try my best to keep my composure
in order to overcome this rush

because this whole thing takes me higher
when I'm kissing your sweet fire

your strawberry
your cherries
your peach and cream

I'm in a fool's paradise
lost in a dream

baby look at me
I take great pleasure in pleasing you

I find incredible pleasure in spoiling you
but I'm curious...

do you ever tell your girlfriends
about the things that I do to you?

One Kiss

4 just one kiss
I'll wait right here
2 touch your sweet sweet lips

for just one night
2 spend the tyme
with you
I'd never miss

2 be with you
I wonder
will it be soon enough

to look into your eyes and make love to you
without the slightest touch

my remaining days would be of joy
my life would be complete

for just one kiss
I'll wait right here
4 u
eternally

You Make Me Feel

I look at you and think of all
the pleasant things I could write about you

all of the emotions in my heart
and mind that you make me feel

those sweet emotions that wander
aimlessly inside of me

they make me feel good all over

you make me feel good all over

you know

Pillow

I'm safe in the darkness
when you're close to me at night

your fragrance on my pillow
makes me want to hold you tight

and quite honestly
I can't sleep sometymes when I'm alone

I don't want to

I can't stay away from you too long

for what I feel for you is real
its written in stone

my room is like a paradise
with you here by my side

it obvious that you feel the same

I can see it in your eyes

and when you whisper in my ear
those sweet words comfort me

together in each others arms
we both fall fast asleep

I Thought About You 2day
I Want U Now

thoughts of you seemed to fill my mind 2day
so I stopped what I was doing
and sat down to reflect on you

I thought about you today

I thought about you when I bought those roses
and before I placed the petals upon the bed
one
by
one

I thought about pouring us
a couple of glasses of champagne
and of how I would pick you up
then lay you down upon the bed

I though about how I would take my tyme to
undress you

piece

by
piece
until all of your clothes were off of you

I thought about taking a rose and touching it
to the side of your neck
your chest
and your breast

just to see if you would like that

I thought about taking an ice cube
and then rubbing it in circles on your nipple
just before I kissed it
so you could feel
the chill of the ice
followed by the warmth of my mouth

I thought about being that summer breeze
that runs free
underneath your dress

that breeze that cools you off
on those nights when you get hot and bothered
and restless

yes restless

I thought about lifting you
from the bed and standing behind you
just a half inch from touching you
and then tracing the length of your bare shoulders
with my finger
right before I placed a delicate kiss
on the back of your neck

and if you wanted to you could close your eyes
then fall back on my chest

then feel my hands moving slowly down the backside
of your arms
down to your forearms
and touching your hands with mine
and locking arms in front of you

and as I continued to stand behind you
holding and embracing you
my extra-extra-large frame protects you

then suddenly I direct my kisses
to the center of your back
soft

gentle
kisses
covering your back
inch
by
delicious
inch

my goodness

so now I'm kissing you until I am down on my knees
at the small of your back
which has suddenly become your front

I thought about sucking that charm
on your stomach chain
before I went further down to your forest
and started sucking again

I thought about sneaking a peak at your facial expression
as I ate you like pieces of mango

I thought about using my tongue
to tickle the bottom of your feet

then spreading your legs
and diving into the moist of your Caramel Sweet

I thought about making you cum
my way
for as long as you would like to go
that way

I thought about taking you pass an orgasm
and beyond the limits of previous pleasures
you've already experienced in the past
like taking you on a journey to the other side
of your deepest secrets

if only you would open up and let me

I thought about getting a little freaky with you
by riding you doggie-style and spanking you on that ass

that is
if you don't mind

and then I could try my best to take your mind away
as you take my mind away

every tyme you touch my skin

every tyme I kiss your face
I thought about the feel of your heart beating
when you lay on top of me

the warmth and the ecstasy
the absolute pleasure of when your soft body completely
surrenders to me

I thought about popping that top
and pouring cool champagne
all over your hot body
and then licking every drop
from every place
on your body

now I must admit
you got me

I can't imagine of any other place that I'd rather be
than with you baby

and that's the reason why
I'm still thinking about you

Your Passion

I hunger for your tender kiss
but what am I to do

I marvel at your elegance
a queen I have in you

I give in to your soft caress
I weaken when you smile

I heat up at your freakiness
your passion drives me wild

your passion drives me
it's your passion

that

drives me

wild

Here And Now
(and until forever)

and still
to this day
I compare her to the beauty
of the rising and setting of the sun
at the beginning and closing of each day

for if I was ever to compose any composition
albeit sincere and from the reaches of mine own heart
and the depths of my soul
I probably would fall short
of expressing how I truly cherish and adore her so

here and now
watching her sleep
under the soft moonlight which covers her body

watching her breathe and dream
and hoping that she might be dreaming of me

looking out into the stars and asking

could she
this woman
truly be for me?

my angel?
my soulmate?

for my soul dances at the mere thought of you
if ever there was such a thing as a *mere* thought of you

and God knows that a man isn't suppose to feel chills
when you rub my skin

and a man isn't suppose to get weak
when you turn my way to kiss me

and a man isn't suppose to shed tears of joy
in his solitude
facing the heavens
falling to his knees and crying
thank you
thank you

thank you
for blessing me

the full moon smiles upon you
and I. . .
I wonder if this may be my last night on earth

I wonder if my life had reached its pinnacle
when I made love to you

for I know not of any other feeling
worth experiencing after loving you

should I fear that God will take my soul 2nite?

or should I clear my mind of such foolish thoughts
and enjoy the hear and now

as dawn appears to chase the stars from the sky
the sunlight enters the room
covering your body

and I sit here
watching you

beautiful you

so again I ask
should I compare you to the beauty
of the rising and falling of the sun
at the beginning and closing of the day

or should I just...

should I just be grateful for you
my love

Chocolate Cookies

(sweeter than a piece of candy)

I dream of being yours
only
completely

I never thought it could happen to me
but ever since my first seeing you
I haven't been the same

and right now there is something I must say to you
and when I'm finished I hope you won't think bad of me

I can't pretend any longer
and now I realize the profound effect
that you have on me

I don't know the reason why
but something happens when you come near me

I can't control it
it just happens

what makes you smile the way you do
you have a smile that I could write
a million romantic verses about

why do you make me feel like this
is it an act?

you probably do this shit on purpose
I'll bet you do don't you?

well let me see
how could I say this poetically ?

when you are near...
or when thoughts of you fill my head I just...

aw fuck it!
come over here before I go out of my mind

just looking at your fine ass makes me want you

thinking about you is foreplay enough for me

move closer to me and take this kiss
softly upon your lips
then over to your cheek
and alongside your neck
you got me licking you now
trying to get you wet?

you got me kissing you
and slipping down onto your shoulder
until I can't kiss no more

but I want you to just lay back and relax
because I've got something else in store

then suddenly I look up to see your nipples standing so
erect on top of your chest
and that's when I wonder
if you can feel the warmth of my mouth
covering them

one
by
one

and stroking them with my tongue

and um so hungry for the left nipple
and if you let me I would indulge myself all night on the
right

then afterwards I journey
sliding a pathway down to your treasure my lips on your
stomach
until I find my way down to that treasure
I wanna
I wanna
I wanna take you to ecstacy
and fill you up with unbelievable pleasure

I wanna have you trembling with joy
I want to make your body shake like a leaf
so spread your legs
don't be afraid
to feel my body heat

can you feel it moving
mouth to mouth

tongue to pearl
a pleasure well received

an indescribable experience
you definitely have to feel
in order to believe

so baby
while I'm here
don't hold back
just do anything you want to do

then drench my face from cheek to cheek
all covered wet with you

now I want you to just let go
because I love to taste your juices flow
and you can rub my head to let me know
how well a job I've done

I'm going to turn you inside out
to prove that I'm the one

your thighs wrapped so tight around my head
I nearly suffocate
then in and out my tongue moves
like when you masturbate

your body trembles with all the joy
and pleasure makes you moan

I'll be as nasty as you want me to be
if I can call you my very own
baby I'll be as nasty as you want me to be

just to make your body quake
as I wanted to do from the start
I'll be as nasty as you want me to be

when I enter you from behind
I hope you won't mind
if I leave fingerprints or little marks
and I promise not spank you too hard
I will only be as nasty as you want me to be

because ain't no mountain high enough when I rise
and ain't no valley low when I'm inside

So put your face in the pillow
to muffle the sounds

lift that ass up in the air
so nice

so round

then off we ride

where we stop no one knows

oh the feel of
the thrill of

the taste of
the touch

I just can't get enough of your

chocolate cookies

So Happy

My heart beats for
the things you give 2 me

unconditional
undying
tender love so sweet

my life revolves around
your love and energy

I know you can tell
how I feel outside

but inside
if you could only see
how happy you've made me

Voyeurism

when u sleep
do u dream of me

I can see you laying there on those red sateen sheets
staring
watching me
as you lay down on that bed

stretching out
closing your eyes and
letting your mind clear for meditation

but first what I want you to do is
see me appear in a vision
a dream-like image
here for you to have you way with me

a voyeur I am in watching you lie there in the nude
and I'm getting off on it

I can't help it

I'm taken by your body
your beautiful naked body

so could you include me in your world?
on your island?
In that place where you dare to satisfy
every sexual impulse you deem necessary to fulfill?

can I be there with you?
can I unbutton my shirt?
its so hott in here you know...
And I'm burning inside!!!

I stand here watching your hands caress your breast
and I like that
I like that a lot

and seeing your nipples rise in excitement
in between your fingers
in response to you licking and playing with them so lovingly

damn I like that

I can see your hands moving

ever so gently between your thighs
yes
in between those thighs

a slight nervousness takes over me
causing me to inhale deeply
from the sight of you toying with your juicy sweet

and I stand here with intentions
to have you in all kind of positions
as you lay there on those sheets

I'm deeply moved by the sight of this erotic performance
that you so boldly display for me
such an arousing scene

it's getting quite warm in here
can I take off my pants?
because they fail to conceal my excitement
as you can clearly see

so now I ask you
are you ready?

are you prepared for me?

if so then you should open your eyes so you can see this
so you can see what you have done to me
you have taken me from the minimum
to the extent of my maximum length

feeling me diving into your depths and widths

as we roll in the constant movements
of my pelvis colliding into your hips

I find that I get harder in the softest part of you

open your eyes and see
the beauty of you and I joined
moving in unity
yes
sweet woman
so sweet

I'm caught up with every single thing you do to me
you release and you receive me completely

and those one thousand positions we perform

stoking each others egos
satisfying the urge to feel you internally
then you respond with a whisper

"Hurt Me..."
and again you speak,

"Hurt Me, Please Hurt..."
and then you open wider for me to get a little more

"Me..."
and I do my damndest to
"Hurt Me"

but this tyme you sound off at a higher pitch
and you feel me go deeper from the rear
as I continue to hear
"Hurt...
Me...
Baby...
Please..."

you sound in a cry-like voice
that echos from the corridors all of your erotic secrets
wanting me to take you to that place of sweet pain

as my pounds and thrusts finds your spot
over and over again
with force my body meets yours
open our eyes

with force I thrust then strike you on the ass
open your eyes baby

open them wide
with force I ride it hard and strong!

baby open yours eyes so you can see
and keep these visions inside of your memory

feel me

watch me
as it sinks
brown muscle in the thickness of pink
taking you beyond limits of ordinary thought

imagine

think

with force your juices flow from your flower
as spring water does in a creek

drenching me

becoming a part of me

now we are
wrapped in each others arms

you and I

complete

so as you lay there on your bed tonight
I want you to see me appear in a dream-like image

here
for you
to have your way
with me

imagine

think

sweet dreams baby

Soul Sista

and I will be alright
as long as I have a soul sista by my side

she holds our future inside her womb
in her embrace there is a tenderness
a warmth

the warmth of a mother
the intelligence of a sista
the personality of a Soul Sista

she's a down
strong
independent sista
with an intelligence that turns me on like a mutha!
be it straight hair
fades
dreads
or even a bald head

from damn near white
to blue black

she keeps me going
she keeps me running back

when she smile
she makes me smile

when she smile
she makes the whole world smile

delicate
she is endeared by real brothers

affectionate
she is the reason the seasons have meaning

compassionate
she forgives me for my bullshit

loving
she takes me back into her welcoming waiting arms

and to me it doesn't get any better than that

she's not behind me
my soul sista is right by my side

no matter what happens to me
she stays right by my side
to whisper an encouraging word like
"baby, it'll be alright"
and sometymes that's all I need to know
for me to keep up the fight

she's that irresistible sista
who abandons the routine of laying on
pound after pound of make-up

she wears those natural scents
not those loud perfumes that aggravate my sinuses
and in my opinion a lot of those perfumes stink

she's that meditating sista
who takes the quiet tyme to find her soul
and that's one of the things I love about her
because finding herself helps her to deal with

others

she's not into a lot of drama

she's intelligent enough to know
what's worth getting excited over

my Soul Sista

when she was a child she did childish things
but now she is a woman

that Soul Sista

the stride in her walk
pure grace

the swaying of her hips
motivates

and through her lips escapes words
in the form of a poem or song
that just so happens to be my favorite poem
and my favorite song

that's why I dare not waist my dreams

on Revlon Queens
and one night flings

I would rather travel your road

and spend my tyme checking you out
wearing those sandals
and that silver ring around your middle toe

I'd like to kiss that toe
but don't tell nobody I said so
let's just keep it on the low

she's that sista who glances my way
and in my head I can hear "Groove With You"
by the Isley Brothers'
or "Distant Lover" by Marvin Gaye

when our spirits meet it gets hotter than an oven
and I ain't ashamed to say that she taught me
good lovin'

she's my all and all
we got each other so she doesn't have to buy
some pet rock

or some damn dog
you see

because I can be her dog if she wants me to be

Sensational Soul Sista
my shining star
my guiding light

a phenomenal thing you truly are
stay right by my side

a masterpiece
a work of art
the center of my universe
my beating heart
my Soul Sista

when she was a child she did childish things
but now she is one badd ass Soul Sista

and I will be aright as long as I have you
here
by my side

The Choice Is Yours

should we choose the sunset
in favor of the sunrise

should we choose the warmth of the summer's breeze
or the chill of the winter's night

should we choose the Indigo horizon
in favor of the star-filled sky

should we ever dream of anything
other than you and I

should we choose the threatening rain clouds
or the calm before the storm

a quiet cabin off in the woods
with a fireplace to keep us warm

should we choose the symphony

or the soothing sounds of jazz

should we get out of the bed this afternoon
or lay back and watch tyme pass

the choice is yours

Did You Like ?
(The Very First Tyme)

I've never tried this before
so please have a little patience with me

um kinda afraid to try it
but I trust you
so I guess its ok

I have been having my doubts
from tyme to tyme
but I've been thinking about it all day

so here we go

kneeling down before you
slowly easing my way in between your thighs

hold on
scoot up just a little baby
ok
ok

I saw you smile then say
go head baby its ok

and in knowing that
I then closed my eyes and took a dive
umm

I heard you make a sound up there
but I was busy down here without a care
rotating my tongue
moving to the left and right
this ain't too badd
in fact its alright

and I'm hoping
by the sounds that you're making
that you like

do you like

now you got me covering you with feather-like strokes
in that area
trying to find that spot that I heard so much about
and in the process
I discover that you really can turn yourself inside out

wow

my lips kissing those lips

cuffing that ass
locking my arms around those hips

I tell you
don't go no where

you tell me
yes baby
stay right there

and I did stay right there

until every star filled the Chicago sky
I stood right there

until tears of joy raced from your weeping eyes
I stood right there

until my mind went blank
and my tongue grew numb
I faithfully stood right there

not only for you
but also for me

you see whenever you and I meet
it doesn't take much

for you bring out the beast in me

you know
the sexual beast
the K-9
the D-O-G

we just have that chemistry
that synergy

well getting back to the story

um on my knees as I bask in the taste your reaction

feeling you tremble
and reaching for things that weren't even there

hearing you mumbling words that sounded like
German mixed with Russian
and a little Ebonics thrown in there too

now I know its not polite to talk with your mouth full
so I'm thinking to myself
this is the shit
and you keep saying
that's it

baby
please
please
don't quit

your
uncontrollable breaths
muscle tightening
your fist balling up
gritting your teeth
blood racing through your veins
your heart pounding
pounding
pound

and you help me get into it
the way that you like it
the way that you like for me to do it
and all I want to be is your willing student of seduction
so let me prove my worth and earn the right to take your
body and mind to extended moments of bliss
but first
baby teach me how to do it right
teach me to please you
teach me to stay my ass down here all night
in between your thighs
because I like
and um hoping that you take delight
when i kiss it light

and tickle it
with my wet tongue swipes

damn baby
you got me to the point where I don't wanna leave this spot

I'm trying my very best to take you there
I'm giving you all I got

let me kiss it again
and let me just touch it once more
let me taste just a little bit again
let me touch and then taste
and kiss it all over again

let me fall into this gap
and stay caught in this trap
because I got a feeling that the sweetness of this Kitt-Kat
will have me coming back

baby I'm starting to like it down here

when you rub my head
does that mean I'm doing it right

when you start pulling hard at my ears
does that mean I'm doing it right baby

when you grind your hips tenderly against my lips
does that mean that I might be taking you on a trip
somewhere
while I'm down there

when it starts to get wetter and wetter and wetter
does that mean I'm doing it just a little better

now this might sound a little crazy but
I heard that the juices make the mustache grow
is that true

let's try something new

straddle my shoulders
um about to pick you up

were going keep doing it while um standing up
don't worry baby
um strong enough see

and when I'm a good boy
you open up and feed me

your warm juices feed me

I'm so hungry for you

open up

and

feed me

Missing You This Summer

in summer's air
I inhaled the warmth
in an attempt at reliving summers past

in summer's sound
the laughter of lovers resound in the back of my mind
just as your laugh used to

in summer's beauty
I marvel at its sight
yes
the way that I still marvel at you
my sweet

I'm missing you this summer

My Brand New Love Seat

I started by walking over to you
as you sat comfortably on the love seat
looking as gorgeous as you wanted

I got down on my knees
took your hand in mine and proceeded to kiss
each and every one of your fingers
one by one

you sat on the edge of the love seat in surprise
before you saw the serious in my eyes

I told you I was gonna get you tonight
you then slid back to relax
at the same tyme lifting up your dress
for me to kiss those kneecaps

my hands caressed the back of your legs
just like in my dream

your skin gave in to my kisses
as my lips pressed softly your thighs

gently your hand stroked the side of my face
and as my tongue danced on your skin
I searched to find that magic place
so you opened wider to let me in

my hands
like spiders climbed up your thighs
you lay your head back
then closed your eyes
took a deep breath and slowly sighed

yeah
I got your ass 2nite

I told you back in June when I first met you
that I was a freak for a chocolate treat
but you held off until September
thought I wouldn't remember
my promise to make that body weak

one of your shoes came off
when you put your leg on the armrest
but you paid it no mind as I took my tyme
driving you crazy down there
keeping it moist and wet

and wet
and wetter than it could possibly get

wetter than the sea of lust
and hotter than the extent of heat

meanwhile my tongue carried on
with a mind of its own
demonstrating proper freak techniques

ooh the sweet taste of caramel was cummin'
when your body began to shake

drowning me into your waterfalls
and your violent ocean waves
the sweet steady flow of your caramel
reminds you that I'm here to please

so turn around baby
I'm ready for you
let me get up off of my knees

brace yourself on the love seat
I suspect that you might like it hard
all you have to do is just say the word

whenever you want me to stop

climb on the love seat and I'm deeper into you
and if you tell me you've been a Badd Girl
I'll spank you

there's no need to put on a front
you've been a Badd Girl haven't you

don't make me get out the handcuffs
just tell me the truth

the more you keep quiet
the harder I'll thrust

so tell me

you've been bad
haven't you

you can tell me
I'll keep it between us

you Badd Girl

Bon Appetite
(The Grocery List)

Strawberries	So nice to watch you eat
Honey	So thick and oh so sweet
Seedless Grapes	Make the fines of all wines
Milk and You	And you its cereal tyme
Whipped Cream	On your special parts
Vanilla Shake	I'll take a large
Caramel	For goodness sake
Candied Yams	How my mama makes
Chocolate Syrup	Makes it all sweet
Raspberry Jam	A tasty treat

Scented Candles	Helps set the mood
A Single Rose	I give 2 you
Hot Body Oil	2 Rub you down
Cantaloupe	Nice and round
Bananas	Eat til your hearts content
Pineapples	Satisfaction's evident
Kiwi Fruit	Does have a use
Cherries	Red or black you just can't lose
Champagne	Fills my mind with ease
Honey Dew	I aim 2 please

With you I'm gonna have a feast

Psychoanalysis 3
(Sweet Pain)

we danced right there in the middle of her living room floor
our bodies swaying to the sound of the conga drums
as we smiled and stared into each others eyes

moving closer 2gether
nice and slow in rhythmic movements
staring into each other's eyes

caught in the slow sultry rhythm of the drumbeat
staring into each other's eyes

staring into each other's eyes
until the music died

and now we stand in the middle of the livingroom
in absolute silence
3 inches from touching
hungry for each other

and suddenly a loud scream escapes from the speaker
followed by the sound of one hundred drums
whistles blowing and warrior

so overcome with lust as we rushed to touch
each other with a burning sexual intensity
as if we were starving or desperate for one another

pulling and tearing at each other's garments
until we both were almost nude
leaving only ripped strands of clothing hanging off of us

I hurried to the dining room
and with one movement of my hand I cleared the table
causing the dishes to crash onto the floor

I then placed her at the center of the table
she spread her legs wide
and I buried my face in her soft wetness

she crossed her legs I palmed her softness
determined to make her wetter

I drenched myself in her juices
almost to the point of suffocation

I rose from the table to catch my wind
snatched her up from her prone position
and we rushed to her bedroom

on the side of the bed I turned her around
bent her forward
she turned her head
looked back at me and said
"Hit it hard, baby"

overwhelmed by the sounds of the Afrikan drum
possessed by my own sexual demons

letting them come out 2nite
letting them have their way 2nite
letting them come out and play 2nite

the loud music played at a fast pace
I continued to bump her from the back
as she met me half way

I placed one hand on the side of her hip
and with the other hand slapped her hard on her

backside
only because she liked it hard

one hard spank on the ass
followed by a smooth caress

she held tight to my right thigh
pulling for me to bring more pain

we continued to ride and
she continued to meet me half way

making a distinct clapping sound
as our bodies continued to collide

then suddenly she began to shake
as she held on even tighter to my thigh
and in return I drilled her with a force that she longed for
obligingly assisting her to reach her peak
taking her to ecstacy
when the music stopped
so did we

because of the loud music
we hadn't noticed that outside it was pouring down rain

I laid down on the bed

she walked over to the balcony doors
opened them wide

and let the 2 am wind rushed inside
filling the room with the summer's breeze
causing the drapes to flap like an angel's wings

she stood there
looking like the Goddess of the night

I lay back focusing my eyes on
the silhouette of her beautiful nakedness

she then returned to the bed
laid down next to me
and wrapped herself in my embrace

and by the sound of the rain falling onto the streets
we both fell fast asleep

Brown Eyes
1999

hey Brown Eyes
in my eyes you stand at the forefront
of the sunset and the sunrise

an Ebony Queen of so many different shades
you are celestial
heaven made

and brown eyes I refuse to pretend
like I don't recognize you

and I'd be remiss if I failed to mention
the magic in your fingertips

the warmth in your embrace
the sweetness in your kiss
and that infectious smile stretched across your face

and its each and every little you do
its your nature

or your very essence that draws me close
close

closer to you

and Brown Eyes
you make my spirits rise
you take me
high

hey Brown Eyes
have you ever taken a midnight stroll
barefoot on the beach

have you ever dreamed of walking the dark side of the
moon?
well I do

I dream of taking your hand and sailing the skies
if only for the moment
if only for a little while

and Brown Eyes
I can see us walking in space
floating
drifting away
to our own paradise
to our very own place

hey Brown Eyes
let me fill your days with white roses and orchids

let me give you all that I could possibly give

until I am no longer able to give

(let me tell you what you do to me)

you take me to levels unparallel
you give me pleasure unmatched by the most intense of
pleasures

you take me beyond the ordinary
where I surpass the supernatural

deeper than the human mind could ever conceive to be
you multiply my imagination then divide it into endless
possibilities

you just walk in and steal my dreams
girl you something else

you then make reality of my fantasies
and it all seems so routine

others fail by far to reach par

and you wonder why my appetite for you is so insatiable

I know I do you no justice when I stop to think of you
and the only words that escape from my mind is
" Damn, she is so fine! "

Brown Eyes
its you who make
inspiration flow in me waves

a tidal wave
or shall I say
a monsoon
soaking me

a hurricane
blowing me
away
blowing me away

blowing me away and making me smile
and I can only surrender to you
when I turn to gaze into your eyes

once again I say
you make my spirits rise
when I gaze into your

your beautiful brown eyes

Vincent Tyler makes his own path!

There are some who write for themselves, as a form of self expression. Others write what they believe people, or a particular audience will make a best seller. Rarely can one expect to find an author who can let himself go while intriguing the audience and making them eager for more. Vincent Tyler has done just that!

A native of Chicago's south side, he has been writing since his early teens. Much of his inspiration stems from his travels in the Carribean, a two-year stay in Europe, and the scenery of Chicago's very own lake shore.

Vincent takes the energy of the moment and then falls into own world of fantasy. Other than performing at his much anticipated book signings, he has appeared at many private engagements. He has also appears for a variety of Book Clubs; locally, as well as nationally.

He has developed quite a following, and in spite of the negative spirits and critics, he continues to stay true to his genre.

Vincent is in the process of completing his follow-up collection of short stories, entitled *"Chocolate Cookies."*

For fan mail or additional copies of this book,
and to book Vincent Tyler for your
Private Party or **Book Club**
send correspondence to:

Vincent Tyler
Rose Petals Publishing
P.O. Box 378373
Chicago, Il 60637

773.651.0631

ChcCookies@aol.com

Visit my web site:

ROSEPETALSPUBLISHING.COM

"Two In The Morning"
(meandmysuga-wugga')

"Chocolate Cookies"
&
"Rose Petals"

Tyler42